Ten Nights' Dreams

A 100TH ANNIVERSARY CELEBRATION

Ten Nights' Dreams

Natsume Soseki

Translation and notes with comments by
Takumi Kashima and Loretta R. Lorenz

Soseki Museum in London

S

Ten Nights' Dreams, July 2000

Originally published in Japanese as *Yumejuya* in 1908

First published in 2000 by Soseki Museum in London
80b, The Chase, London SW4 0NG England
e-mail: Nsoseki@aol.com
http://www.dircon.co.uk/soseki-museum/info.html

Print information available on the last page.

ISBN: 978-1-5521-2395-9 (sc)
ISBN: 978-1-4122-4129-8 (e)

Trafford rev. 07/28/2023

 www.trafford.com

North America & international
toll-free: 844-688-6899 (USA & Canada)
fax: 812 355 4082

Contents

Introduction   by Takumi Kashima   vi

Ten Nights' Dreams   by Natsume Soseki   1

Notes   by Takumi Kashima   46

Introduction

Natsume Soseki (1867-1916) is a novelist and scholar of English literature. He ranks with Mori Ogai (1862-1922) as a major figure in modern Japanese literature. Among his works, *Wagahai wa Neko de Aru* (I Am a Cat) and *Botchan* (Master Darling) are especially known to almost every Japanese and are read even by primary school pupils. His portrait is printed on the Japanese 1,000-yen note.

Soseki was sent to England as a government-sponsored student when he was a teacher at the Fifth Higher School in Kumamoto Prefecture. It was at the time that Japan gave up its national isolation policy and was emerging as a modern state.

He experienced this historical turning point during his stay in London. On arriving in London, one of the first things he saw was the returning soldiers from the Boer War being mobbed in the streets. One year later began the twentieth century and the British Empire faced the death of Queen Victoria. In 1902 Japan and Great Britain signed the Anglo-Japanese Alliance.

A sense of skepticism toward the progress of civilization was fostered by Soseki's reading of Karl Marx's *Das Kapital,* among other things. His interest in natural science arose through his friendship in London with a Japanese scientist, Ikeda Kikunae.

He was in a position to compare the states of two different nations and to see the Japanese civilization from another perspective. When he began writing novels, his experience in England was naturally reflected in his works.

On returning home, he replaced Lafcadio Hearn at the First Higher School and at Tokyo Imperial University where he lectured on literary theory. Eventually he gave up teaching and began writing for the *Asahi Shimbun* where he spent many years before his death.

Ten Nights' Dreams is a collection of ten short stories or dreams. Among the ten nights, the first, second, third, and fifth nights start with the same sentence, "This is the dream I dreamed." Each dream has a surrealistic atmosphere. Some are funny, and and others are grotesquely weird. For example, in The Third Night, the man carrying his baby on his back turns out to have been a murderer.

Did Soseki try to express what he actually dreamed? Or was his subconscious emerging spontaneously in the form of narrative dream? Whether Soseki actually had these dreams or whether they were complete fictions is not certain. According to notes that he made in 1907 or 1908, Soseki jotted down things that later appear in *Ten Nights' Dreams*. It is said that some comments from these notes were used in the first, third, fourth, seventh, eighth, and tenth Nights.

On May 18, 1908, he wrote a letter addressed to one of his disciples, Komiya Toyotaka, telling him that he was going to write some short stories. This referred either to *Ten Nights' Dreams* or to *Eijitsu Shohin* (Small Works in Spring). At the beginning of the same letter, Soseki said, "What a strange dream you dreamed! I wish you wouldn't write to me about your dreams," though it is possible that some of the dreams originated with Komiya.

In his letter to Takahama Kiyoshi (known as Takahama Kyoshi), Soseki wrote, "I am going to write a series of short stories, entitled *Ten Nights' Dreams*. I will send the first draft to Osaka (i.e. the Osaka *Asahi Shimbun*) today. It is a short affair. I hope you will read it." The letter was dated July 1, 1908, and soon thereafter "The First Night" appeared in the Tokyo *Asahi Shimbun* on July 25.

"The First Night" came out in the Tokyo *Asahi Shimbun* on July 25, 1908 and on the following day in the Osaka *Asahi Shimbun*. Since July 27, when "The Second Night" appeared in both the Osaka and Tokyo *Asahi Shimbun*, Soseki's dreams appeared daily except on August 1, the last one appearing on August 5.

Soseki's *Ten Nights' Dreams* was collected in a separate volume named *"Mura-Kumo"* (A Cluster of Clouds or Gathering Clouds) and published on February 5, 1909. On May 15, 1910, Shunyodo Publishing Company gathered Soseki's four works, *Buncho* (Paddybird), *Eijitsu Shohin*, *Man Kan Tokoro Dokoro* (Travels in Manchuria and Korea), and *Ten Nights' Dreams*, and published them as *"Shihen"* (Four Works).

Soseki's Chronological Table and His Major Works

1867 (Keio 3)
Born as the eighth and last child of Natsume Kohyoe Naotsuka and his wife, Chie. Real name, Kinnosuke. Sent to a foster family immediately after birth and adopted into the Shiobara family.

1876 (Meiji 9)
Back to his parents and the house where he was born. (Returned to original family register, 1888.)

1881 (Meiji 14)
Mother Chie died. Transferred from Tokyo First Junior High School to Nishogakusha and studied Chinese poetry.

1889 (Meiji 22)
Got acquainted with Masaoka Shiki who taught him Haiku (a Japanese poetry form of seventeen syllables).

1890 (Meiji 23)
Entered Tokyo Imperial University and majored in English literature.

1893 (Meiji 26)
Graduated. Appointed lecturer at Tokyo Higher Normal School.

1895 (Meiji 28)
Taught at Matsuyama Junior High School, Ehime Prefecture.

1896 (Meiji 29)
Taught at the Fifth Higher School in Kumamoto Prefecture. Married Nakane Kyoko.

1900 (Meiji 33)
Went to England as a government-sponsored student.

1903 (Meiji 36)
Returned to Tokyo. Replaced Lafcadio Hearn at the First Higher School and at Tokyo Imperial University. Suffered from numerous nervous disorders.

1905 (Meiji 38)
Published *Wagahai wa Neko de Aru* (I Am a Cat); *Rondon To* (The Tower of London)

1906 (Meiji 39)
Botchan (Master Darling)
Kusamakura (The Three-Cornered World)
Nihyakutoka (The Two-hundred-and-tenth Day)

1907 (Meiji 40)
Gave up teaching and wrote for the *Asahi Shimbun* newspaper.
Gubijinso (The Poppy)

1908 (Meiji 41)
Kofu (The Miner)
Yumejyuya (Ten Nights' Dreams)
Sanshiro; part of Soseki's Trilogy.

1909 (Meiji 42)
Sorekara (And Then); known as Soseki's Trilogy.

1910 (Meiji 43)
Suffered bleeding from a gastric ulcer at Shuzenji spa and remained in bed until the following year.
Mon (The Gate); known as Soseki's Trilogy.
Omoidasukotonado (Recollections)

1911 (Meiji 44)
Declined an offer of doctorate by Tokyo Imperial University.

1912 (Taisho 1)
Higansugimade (To the Spring Equinox and Beyond)

1913 (Taisho 2)
Kojin (The Wayfarer)

1914 (Taisho 3)
Kokoro (The Heart)

1915 (Taisho 4)
Michikusa (The Grass on the Wayside)

1916 (Taisho 5)
Meian (Light and Darkness)
Died of gastric ulcer on December the ninth.

The First Night

This is the dream I dreamed.

I was sitting at her bedside with my arms folded. The woman lying on her back said quietly that she was going to die. Her long hair lay on the pillow softly framing her oval face. There was a warm flush on her white cheeks and her lips were, of course, red. She scarcely seemed about to die. But the woman said quietly and clearly that she was going to die. I began to think she would indeed die, so I looked down into her face and asked her plainly if she was really going to die. The woman said she was and opened her eyes wide. Her eyes were charming, deep black ringed by long lashes. I found, reflected clearly at the bottom of those black pupils, myself.

I saw their dark lustre, almost transparent, and found myself still wondering if she would actually die. I bent close to her and asked again, politely, if she would die, and I asked her if she was all right. The woman, opening her dark sleepy eyes wide, said in a low voice she would indeed die and that there was no way out.

Well, then. I asked her attentively if she could see me. She smiled and said I was reflected there. Without a word, I drew my face from the pillow. I sat there, my arms folded, wondering again if she would die.

After a while, the woman spoke again.

"If I die, please bury me yourself. Dig the grave with a large pearl oyster shell. Put a fragment of a fallen star on my grave as a tombstone. Then wait for me there. By and by I will come to see you."

I asked her when.

"The sun rises. And the sun sets. And the sun rises and sets... When the red sun rises in the east and sets in the west, then I will... Will you wait for me?"

I nodded. Her voice became louder and she said with decision, "Wait for me for a hundred years. Sit at my graveside and wait for me one hundred years and I will surely come to see you."

I told her I would wait. I saw my reflection, so clear in her black pupils before, begin to grow hazy and distorted. Still water replaced the moving shadowy reflection. The eyes closed. From beneath the long lashes tears rolled down her cheeks... She was dead.

I went out into the garden and began to dig the grave with a pearl oyster shell. The shell was sharp with a smoothed edge. Moonlight played on the inside of the shell with each scoop of the damp-smelling earth until the grave was dug. I laid the woman inside. Then I spread the soft soil over her. Moonlight played on the inside of the shell each time I smoothed down the earth. I picked up a fragment of a fallen star and placed it gently on the grave. It had an oval shape. I supposed that its long course through the night sky had worn away its sharp edges into the oval. When I held it and arranged it on the soil, I felt my hands and my heart become a little warmer.

I sat on the mossy ground, my arms folded, and wondered if I would wait for her this way a hundred years, gazing at the rounded tombstone. Meanwhile, the sun rose in the east, as the woman had said. It was a large, red sun, and as the woman had said, it set in the west. It dropped suddenly, still red. I counted one.

After a short time, the red sun rose again impassively and set again silently. I counted two.

It was impossible to keep track of how many I had seen. Countless red suns passed over my head, but still the hundredth year did not come. In the end, seeing the rounded stone, now covered with moss, I thought the woman had deceived me.

At last, a green stalk sprouted and began to grow, slanting towards me from under the stone. In an instant it was almost long enough to reach me and stopped just at my chest. At the top of the long straight stalk, an oblong bud hanging at a slight angle, came into flower. It was a white lily and had a strong fragrance. As dew from the heavens fell upon it, the flower nodded under its weight. I put my head forward and kissed the dewy white petals. I drew back. And when I looked at the distant sky, only one star was twinkling in the dawning.

"One hundred years have passed." That was when I first realized it.

The Second Night

This is the dream I dreamed.

I had just left a monk's room and was returning along the passage to my own room. When I entered, a paper-covered lamp was burning dimly on its stand. I knelt with one knee on the cushion and stirred the lamp wick. A flowery piece of blackened wick fell on the vermilion-lacquered stand as the room suddenly brightened.

The picture on the sliding fusuma door was Buson's brushwork. Black willows were drawn thick and dark in the foreground, fading to light in the background. A fisherman looked cold as he walked along a river bank, bamboo hat tilted. A scroll hung on the wall, depicting the figure of Kaichumonju, the Bodhisattva, floating in the sky. The smell of smouldering incense lingered in the dark shadows. It was a vast temple where deep silence prevailed, with no sign of life. An upward glance revealed the round shade of the lamp

5

in fluid reflection on the ceiling, as though alive.

Still kneeling there on one knee, I turned up the cushion with my left hand and felt under it with my right. The dagger was there, as I had expected. Relieved, I turned back the cushion and sat down with a thud.

"Aren't you a Samurai? As a Samurai you are supposed to attain spiritual enlightenment," the monk had sneered. "You have never once been able to contemplate, have you? You certainly are no Samurai. More like the dregs of mankind, I would say. Ha! You look angry." He laughed scornfully. "I dare you to bring me proof that you have achieved contemplation." He looked away abruptly. Insufferable.

"I will attain spiritual enlightenment by the time the clock in the adjoining hall strikes. Once I've attained it, I'll go again to the priest's room, this very night. I'll exchange my enlightenment for his life. But not until I am spiritually awakened can I take his life. I must achieve this. I am a Samurai."

"If I do not succeed in contemplation tonight, I will end my life. How can a Samurai live who is humiliated? I will kill myself once and for all."

In this vein of thought, my right hand slid unconsciously under the cushion and I pulled out the vermilion-lacquered sheath with my dagger inside. I held it a moment, drew my breath, and whipped out the little sword. The cold blade shone in the dark room. My hand let a horrible whistling stroke escape through the air. I held the dagger at arm's length and concentrated my whole being on the tip of its blade. I was livid with hate. I seemed to see the dagger shrink, as through a convex glass, to a mere needle in my hand, and I felt an intense need to stab. It was as though every drop of my blood had surged into that right wrist. My hand holding the dagger was wet with perspiration. I felt my lips quiver.

I sheathed the knife and drew it to my right side. Then I sat down cross-legged on the cushion. The famous master Joshu says, "Nothingness..." "What is nothingness? The silly old ass."

I clenched my jaw and let out the warm breath through my nostrils. My temples felt taut and throbbed with pain. I opened my eyes until they bulged to twice their size.

I saw the wall-hanging. I saw the paper-covered lamp. I saw the tatami mat of straw. I saw the monk's bald head clearly. I heard him laugh as he opened his cavernous mouth. To hell with him! I must dismiss him from this world, no matter what. I will. I surely will attain complete enlightenment. I kept my mind set on nothing. No word crossed my mind, but I could still smell the damned incense.

Suddenly I clenched my fist and struck myself on

the top of the head as hard as I could. I ground my teeth. Sweat poured from under my arms. My back stiffened. I felt a sudden pain in my knees. "Let them break." But it was excruciating. Intense revulsion came over me. "I cannot reach the state of nothingness." Whenever I felt I was about to reach it, the pain seemed to become more intense, bringing me back. I felt anger. I felt regret. I felt deep chagrin at my failing attempt. Tears flowed from my eyes. I thought of throwing myself on a big rock and smashing my flesh and bones to bits.

But I remained sitting patiently. I had to endure this gut-rending sorrow. It swelled in all my muscles and tried to gush out through the pores of my skin, but they were tightly closed. There was no relief, no mercy.

During all this, I seem to be someone else. I feel there is no paper-covered lamp, no brush painting by Buson, no tatami, no alcove with shelves, though they once seemed to exist. Yet they would not really disappear. I just keep sitting in the prescribed position. It comes suddenly, the clock in the adjoining hall, sounding its first stroke.

I come to myself with a start. I am clutching my dagger in my right hand. The clock strikes for the second time.

The Third Night

This is the dream I dreamed.

I was walking, with a six-year-old child on my back. I was sure he was my son, but oddly enough, I didn't know why he was blind and bald-headed like a bonze priest. I asked him when he had become blind and he answered that he had been so for a long time. His voice was childlike, but he spoke like a mature man with no respect for his father.

We were on a long footpath crossing a field of young rice. Sometimes a snowy heron would glance against the darkness.

"We have come to the rice field, I guess," the boy on my back said.

"How do you know?" I asked him, turning my head back toward him.

"I know by the heron's shriek."

Then a heron's cry sounded twice just as he had said.

9

I began to feel afraid of him even though he was my son. With this weird creature on my back, I felt something horrible was about to happen to me. I looked around for some good place to throw this creature away. There was a big wood ahead in the darkness. I thought it might be a good place to do that, and then I heard a snicker from behind me.

"Why are you laughing?" I asked him. There was no answer to my question. Instead he said, "Am I heavy for you, Father?" I answered no. And he said, "I think I will be heavier soon."

I kept walking, aiming wordlessly at the woods. The path kept winding through the fields, so it was difficult to get out. After a while I came to a point where the lane forked. I stopped there to take a little rest.

"You should find a stone marker here," the child said. It was true. I could see a square-shaped stone pillar of about eight by eight inches. It stood as high as my waist. It said to go left to Hidarigakubo and right to Hottahara. I could see the red characters on the stone very clearly in the dark. They were scarlet like the stomach of a newt.

"You'd better go to the left," the boy told me. I looked over to the left and saw the woods I was aiming at casting dark shadows over us. I hesitated a little.

"What are you waiting for?" The boy urged me again. I reluctantly took the way in the direction of the woods. I kept walking on and on along the lane leading to the woods, wondering how he could know everything in spite of his blindness.

"I hate being blind. It's so troublesome," he said at my back.

"That's why I'm carrying you on my back. That should make you feel better."

"I'm grateful to you for carrying me on your back, but people make a fool of me for being blind. Even my father does."

I became disgusted with this boy and hurried to leave him in the woods as soon as possible.

"Just a little further and you will find out something. I remember it happened on just this sort of night," he said at my back as though he were talking to himself.

"What are you talking about?" I asked him sharply.

"Why do you ask? You know very well," the child answered scornfully. Then I felt I knew something, though I wasn't quite sure what it was. And I felt I knew it had actually happened on this sort of night. A little further might lead me to more certainty. But something warned me that I might be better off not knowing what it was. I had to get rid of him as soon as possible before I found out. I quickened my pace still more.

It had been raining for some time. With each step, it got darker. I tried to concentrate on going forward. The boy stuck to my back was reflecting, like a mirror, every tiny thing in my past, present, and future. And he was my own child, who was blind. I couldn't stand it any more.

Just then I heard, "Here! Here, right at the bottom of that cedar tree!"

His voice sounded very clearly in the rain. I stopped unconsciously. I had come into the woods before I knew it. There was something black about six feet ahead. It looked like a cedar tree, as he had said.

jizo

"Father, you did it at the bottom of that cedar tree; you remember?"

"Yes, that's where I did it," I answered in spite of myself.

"It was in the 5th year of Bunka (1808), the year of the Dragon, wasn't it?" I thought he was right.

"So it is just 100 years since you killed me here!"

As soon as I heard these words, I knew suddenly I had killed a blind man on this sort of night at the bottom of that same cedar tree 100 years ago, in the 5th year of Bunka, the year of the Dragon. And when I realized for the first time that I was a murderer, suddenly the little one on my back became much heavier than before, like a jizo stone child.

The Fourth Night

There was a long table on the large earthen floor. Around the table some small folding chairs were set. The table was black and shiny. At one corner of the table there was an old man drinking, with a square tray in front of him. He seemed to be drinking sake and eating nishime, simmered vegetables, from the tray.

His face was very pink from drinking, and his complexion smooth and unwrinkled. Only his long beard told me that he was an old man. Being a little child, I wondered how old he was. Then a woman came from the backyard, bringing water in a bucket from

nishime

the well. She asked him, wiping her hands on her apron, "How old are you?" The old man swallowed a mouthful of nishime and answered affectedly, "I forget how old I am." The woman was standing, looking at his face crossly with her hands in her thin sash. The old man drank some hot sake in one gulp, in a cup as big as a rice bowl, and let out a long breath through his white beard. Then the woman asked him, "Where do you live?" The old man stopped in mid-breath and said, "I live in the depths of the navel." The woman asked him again, keeping her hands in the sash, "Where are you going?" The old man drank more hot sake at one draught from the big cup and blew a long breath as before, and said, "Somewhere." "And are you going straight there?" the woman asked, and then the deep breath he let out passed through the shoji, the sliding screen of paper, under the leaves of a willow tree and went straight to the riverside.

The old man went out. I went out after him. A small gourd was swinging at his waist. He was carrying a square box under his arm that hung from his shoulder by a cord. He was wearing a pair of bluish lightweight pants and a sleeveless shirt of the same colour. Only his socks were yellow. They looked like leather.

The old man went directly to the willow tree near the river and stood under it. There were some children there. He drew part of a bluish towel out of his pants, laughing. He twisted it lengthwise as though he were making a paper rope. Then he put the twisted towel down on the ground and drew a circle around it. To finish his work, he took out a candy-man's brass whistle from the box hanging on his shoulder.

He said, "Keep your eyes on the towel, keep your eyes on the towel, soon it will be metamorphosed into a snake." He said this again and again. The children stared at the towel in the circle eagerly. I stared at it, too.

"Keep your eyes on the towel, keep your eyes on the towel. All right?" he said and began to walk around the circle blowing the whistle. I kept staring closely at the towel, but it didn't move at all.

The old man kept blowing the whistle and walking around the circle. He kept turning, walking on tiptoe in his straw sandals, as though sneaking. It looked as if he were afraid of the towel and was taking care not to wake it up. He looked afraid, and at the same time interested.

straw sandals

After a while the old man stopped blowing the whistle. He opened the box suspended from his shoulder, picked up an end of the towel and threw it into the box.

"Leave it alone for a while and it will become a snake. I will show you the snake soon, very soon," he said and began to walk away in a straight line. He passed through the willow branches and went straight down the path. I wanted to see the snake, so I went after him all the way. He kept walking, sometimes saying, "It will wake" or "It will be a snake." In the end he came to the river, singing.

"Soon it will wake,
To be a snake.
Surely it will;
The whistle will trill."

I thought he would take a rest there and show me the snake in the box because there was no bridge or boat around. But he continued going straight and began to splash across the river. His knees, waist, and breast gradually disappeared in the water. The old man still made his way straight through the river, singing.

"The river will deepen.
The day will darken.
The world will straighten its path."

Finally his beard, head, and hood all disappeared

17

into the water.

I still thought he would show me the snake after he got to the opposite side of the river, so I kept waiting and waiting for him to come up again, standing alone hearing the reeds singing in the wind. But the old man never came up again.

The Fifth Night

This is the dream I dreamed.

It seemed to be a time long gone by, an age as old as the gods. I had been fighting in some unknown war, but had suffered an unlucky defeat and had been captured alive. I was grabbed and forced to sit down in front of the enemy captain.

People in those days were all tall; and they all wore long beards. Each wore a girdle of leather and carried a saber that looked like a stick. Their bows seemed to have been fashioned from thick wisteria vine, neither lacquered nor polished, very simple.

The enemy captain was sitting on what looked like an earthenware vessel turned upside-down, with his bow in his right hand. When I looked at his face, I saw bushy eyebrows that met over the bridge of his nose. There were no razors at that time, of course.

As a captive, I was not allowed to be seated on a bench or chair, so I sat cross-legged on the grass. I

19

was wearing big straw boots. The boots at that time reached right up to the knees. The front and back seams were left unwoven and the straw was gathered into ornamental tufts that swung with every step.

The captain scrutinized my face in the firelight and asked me if I would live or die. It was the custom in those days to ask a captive that question. To answer that one would live meant submission; that one would die meant no surrender at any cost. I answered shortly. "Die." The captain threw aside the bow which stuck in the grass, and unsheathed the stick-like sword slung from his waist. The flames bowed and bent before the winds that blew against the sword. I opened my right hand like a maple and raised my palm over my eyes, the signal for the captain to wait. He returned the sword to its scabbard.

Even that long ago there were such things as love affairs. I told him that I wanted to see my woman once again before I died. He said he would wait until the cock crowed at daybreak. I had to get my woman here before the cock crowed, or die without seeing her.

The captain sat staring into the bonfire. I waited for her, cross-legged in my big straw boots there on the grass. The night went on.

I sometimes heard a branch in the bonfire give

way. Every time, the flaming branch would detach itself and fall, scattering a shower of sparks over the captain's figure. His eyes glittered under the black brows. Someone came and threw an armful of new branches into the fire. After a little while the fire would crackle, sounding brave enough to snap back at the darkness.

My woman led out the white horse from the back where it had been tethered to an oak. She passed her hand over its mane three times, and sprang on to its back. The horse was bare-backed, with neither saddle nor stirrup. When she kicked its belly with her long white legs, the horse darted forward at a full gallop. As someone added more firewood, the sky far beyond began to show a faint light. The horse seemed to breathe shafts of fire from its nostrils as it flew through the darkness toward the dawn. The woman kicked ceaselessly with her slender legs. Her hair flew like a long tail behind her in the darkness. And yet the bonfire was a long way off.

Just then at the side of a dark road she heard a cock crowing its long warning of the dawn. She pulled up the reins. The horse pawed the hard rock with its fore hooves, a sharp, ringing sound.

The cock crowed a second time, raising its high-pitched cry.

She let out the tightened reins in a rush and the

horse fell to its knees, pitching forward with its rider atop. Below them lay a deep abyss.

The hoof prints still remain gouged into the rock. It was Amanojaku, the nymph of perversity, who had imitated the crowing cock. As long as those hoof prints remain there, she is my sworn enemy.

The Sixth Night

I had heard that the great Unkei was carving the figures of the two Temple Guardians, the ancient Nio, at the main gate of Gokoku Temple, so I walked out to see it. There were many people already there before me all talking about the project.

Before the main gate stood a red pine tree five or six *ken* high (about ten meters), spreading its branches out against the blue sky far above, at an angle that partially screened its roof. The green of the pine tree and the vermilion of the lacquered gate reflected each other in beautiful harmony. The tree was well placed so that one heavy branch extended obliquely to avoid blocking the left side of the gate. It seemed somehow old-fashioned to let the branch stick out over the roof that way. It could have been the Kamakura Period.

However, the people looking at it, including me, were of the Meiji era. Most of them were rickshaw drivers. They must have been standing there because they were tired of waiting for passengers.

One said, "That's what I call big!"

"That must be harder than it is to make a man," said another.

Still another said, "Do they still carve the Nio nowadays? I thought that was all way back when."

"It looks plenty strong all right. They say there was never anyone as strong as the Nio. They say they were even stronger than Yamato-takeru-no-mikoto, that ancestor-god of the emperor himself." This speaker with his kimono tucked in was not wearing a hat. He seemed somewhat uncultured.

Unkei was working with his chisel and hammer, unconcerned about his reputation among the onlookers. He never turned to look at them. Perched on his high place, he went on carving the first Nio.

Unkei was wearing the strange headgear of a bygone era and had his sleeves tied across his back. Anyway, his whole aspect was that of another age. He seemed to be ill-matched with his noisy audience. It was strange to be watching him there. I wondered why he was still alive in this modern period.

Unkei, however, was carving away as if everything were absolutely normal. A young man who was looking up at him turned to me and began extolling his work, saying, "He is great. We are beneath his notice. He seems to be telling us that he and the Nio are the world's only heroes. I think he is splendid."

I thought that his words were interesting. I glanced at him and he said at once, "Look how he uses the chisel and hammer. That's exquisite mastery."

He was now carving the Nio's eyebrow a *sun* (3.03 cm) sideways, and in the precise instant that he turned over the blade of the chisel, he brought the hammer down. He planed the hard wood and thick shavings flew with the sound of the hammer as the side of an angry nose emerged. He seemed to have an unconcerned way of working, yet his hand was perfectly sure.

"He uses the chisel in such an offhand manner. How can he make the eyebrows and nose the way he wants?" I was so impressed that I began talking to myself. "No," the young man at my side observed. "He doesn't do it with his chisel. All he does is just dig out the eyebrows and nose already buried in the wood. It's like digging stones out of the ground. He cannot make a mistake."

What a discovery. So this is what sculpture is! It occurred to me that if that is all there is to it, anybody can do it. I suddenly longed to make a statue of the Nio for myself, so I went off home there and then.

I got the chisel and hammer out of my toolbox. In the backyard there was a large stack of oak wood, already sawed up for firewood after a recent storm had scattered tree branches about.

I chose the biggest one and began to carve it vigorously, but unfortunately I couldn't seem to find the Nio. I couldn't find one in the next piece, either. Nor was it in the third. I carved into the stacked wood piece after piece, but in none was hidden the Nio. At last I had to accept the fact that the Nio does not reside in the wood of the Meiji period. I also learned the reason why Unkei is alive today.

The Seventh Night

I find myself on board an extraordinarily big ship. The ship steams against the waves emitting black smoke continuously day and night and making a deafening noise. The trouble is, I have no idea where the ship is heading. The sun, reflected like burning tongs, seems to come from beneath the waves. I see the sun motionless above the tall mast for a time, but in the next moment it passes the big ship and finally disappears again into the depths, sputtering on the water as though the burning tongs had been suddenly dropped there. Each time this happens, blue waves turn blackish-red far beyond and the ship makes a terrible noise in a vain chase after the sun's traces.

Once I got hold of a crewman on deck. "Is this ship heading west?"

The man glared at me for a moment. "Why?" He finally asked.

"Because the ship seems to be running after the

setting sun," I replied.

The man gave a loud, amused laugh and went off. I heard the strains of a sea shanty:

"Is the Sun heading East? It may be, Ho!
Is its home in the West? Don't ask me, Ho!
It's a sailor I am and belong to the waves;
My ship is my home and ever I roam,
Sail on, sail on, sail on, Ho!"

I came to the forecastle deck and found a crowd of sailors hauling the big jib rope.

I felt completely lost, abandoned. I had no idea when I would be able to get off this ship. I didn't even know where it was heading. I was only sure the ship was steaming ahead against the waves, emitting its black smoke. The waves were fairly high and looked infinitely blue. The water sometimes turned purple, but white foam was always being blown back in the ship's wake. I felt completely lost. I thought of jumping into the sea to my death rather than staying on this ship.

There was a lot of company on board. Most people looked foreign, with very different types of features. As the ship pitched in the heavy, cloudy weather, I found a woman leaning against the rail, crying unceasingly. The handkerchief she used to wipe her tears looked white, I saw, but she wore printed Western clothes, probably cotton. When I looked at her, I realized that I was not the only one who was sad.

One night when I was alone on deck watching the stars, a foreigner came up and asked me if I knew any astronomy. Here I was almost ready to kill myself as a non-entity. What did I need to know about astronomy? But I kept silent. The foreign man began to tell me about the seven stars over Taurus. He said that the stars and the sea were something God had created. Finally he asked me if I believed in God. I just kept silent, looking up at the sky.

Going into the saloon one time, I saw a young woman dressed in flashy clothes. She had her back to me and was playing the piano. Beside her was a tall, fine gentleman singing a song. His mouth looked enormous. Anyway, the man and woman appeared to be entirely indifferent to everyone but each other. They even seemed to have forgotten that they were on a ship.

I found myself getting more and more unhappy. In the end, I decided I would kill myself. One night when there was no one about, I ventured to throw myself into the sea, but just as my feet left the deck and my tie with the ship was severed, I wished from the bottom of my heart that I had not done this thing, but it was too late. I had to enter the sea whether I liked it or not. The ship was so tall that although I was physically parted from it, my feet would not touch the water that quickly, but with nothing to hold on to, it was getting closer and closer. However tightly I curled my legs under me, it was useless. The water was black.

The ship passed me, trailing its perpetual black smoke. I realized that it would have been better for me to stay on board even without knowing where the ship was bound, but I was unable to put this new wisdom to any practical use. I fell deep into the black waves quietly, with infinite regret and fear.

The Eighth Night

As I crossed the threshold into the barber shop, I saw several people there, all dressed in white, who asked in chorus if they might help me.

I stood in the middle of the room, looking around. It was square. The windows on two sides were open and on the other two walls hung mirrors. I counted six mirrors.

I went to one of the mirrors and eased myself deep into a facing chair, which wheezed pleasantly as my body sank into it. It was quite a comfortable piece of furniture to recline in. I saw my face resplendent in the mirror. Behind it there was reflected a window, and slantwise I could see the lattice-work that separated the cashier's counter from the rest of the shop. Behind it there was no one to be seen. Outside the window I could see reflected clearly the upper halves of the passers-by.

Shotarou walked by with a woman. He had bought

a panama hat which we all took no notice of, and he was wearing it. I wonder when he met that woman. I have no idea of such things. Both of them looked proud of being seen together. I wanted to have a close look at the woman's face, but I missed my chance as they had already passed by.

A soybean-curd maker passed blowing on his horn, his lips on the mouth-piece, his cheeks puffed out as if he had been stung by a swarm of bees. I could not help worrying about the man and is puffed cheeks. It looked as though he had spent his whole life being stung by bees.

A geisha came up.

shimada

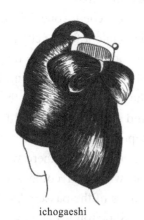

ichogaeshi

She had not yet put on her make-up. Her hair was done up in a loose root of shimada knot, which made it look wobbly on top. She

32

looked sleepy, too. A pity her complexion was so extremely bad. She made a bow and introduced herself to someone, but the person was out of range of the mirror.

Then a big fellow dressed in white stepped up behind me with a pair of scissors and a comb in his hands and began to scrutinize my face. Twisting my thin moustache, I asked him if anything could be done with it. The man in white made no answer, patting my head with the dark brown comb.

I said, "Listen, aside from the matter of my head, will this moustache ever amount to anything?" Still without a word, he began to snip at my hair with the scissors.

I tried to keep my eyes open to see everything reflected in the mirror, but I soon closed them because black hairs began flying to and fro and every snip frightened me. The man in white finally said in a loud voice, "Did you see the goldfish vendor outside, sir ?"

I said I hadn't. The man in white did not ask me anything further and continued busily trimming my hair. I suddenly heard somebody bellow, "Watch out!" I opened my eyes to glimpse the spokes of a bicycle wheel visible from just under the man's white sleeve. The steering wheel of a rickshaw cart appeared. Just then the man in white took my head in both hands and turned it forcefully to one side. The bicycle and the rickshaw snapped out of sight. The sound of snipping was all that could be heard.

The man in white soon came around to my side and started cutting the hair around my ear. I was relieved to open my eyes now that the hairs were no longer flying about. "Awa rice cake; rice cake; rice cake," somebody chanted outside. They were making rice cakes, beating out a rhythm with a small mallet against the large wooden mortar. I would like to have had a look at how they were going about it. The last time I had seen Awa rice cake making had been when I was a small boy. The Awa rice maker, however, never appeared in the mirror. I could only hear the sound.

awa rice cake

I peered as hard as I could into the mirror, trying to see inside, beyond the corner of its frame. I saw a woman whom I had not noticed until then. She was a big dark woman with bushy eyebrows. Her hair was done in the ginkgo style and she was wearing only a lined kimono with a black satin decorative collar as she sat on the mat with one knee up, counting bills. The bills looked like ten-yen ones. The woman was counting intensely, eyes down and thin lips drawn tightly. She certainly worked up speed. She acted as though she was going to count bills forever. Yet the number of bills on her knee was only a hundred at most; however much she counted them they would never amount to more.

I was gazing absently at the woman's face and at the bills. Just then the man in white announced loudly in my ear, "I will wash your hair." It was a good moment to have a direct look at the scene, so as soon as I stood up from the chair I turned around toward the lattice. But nothing, neither the woman nor the bills, could be seen.

I paid and went out, whereupon I found about five oblong basins lined up to the left of the entrance. In them were a lot of goldfish-red ones, spotted ones, lean ones, fat ones. The goldfish seller sat behind the tubs. His eyes were fixed on the goldfish before him. He remained still with his chin resting on his hands. He hardly cared about the busy people passing by. For a little while I stood looking at this goldfish seller, but all that time he didn't move at all.

The Ninth Night

The world has somehow become unsettled. A battle may break out at any moment. There is panic in the air, as though an unbridled horse has plunged wildly from a burning stable and is day and night running amok, round and round the house and grounds,

torii

raucous grooms in pursuit. Yet within the house all was still.

In the house were a young mother and a three-year-old child. The father had gone away somewhere. It was on a midnight dark and moonless that the father had gone away. He had put on straw sandals and his black hood as he sat on the bed, and then he had left by the backdoor. The flame of the lantern that the mother held cut a narrow strip of light into the thick darkness and shone momentarily on an old cypress tree by the hedge.

The father had not returned since that time. Every day the mother would ask the three-year-old child, "Where is Father?" At first the child would not

shrine

answer, but then would say, "Over there." Even when the mother asked, "When will Father be back home?" The child only smiled and again answered, "Over there." Then the mother would smile, too. The mother tried again and again to teach the child the words, "Father will be back in a minute." However, the child only learned to repeat, "In a minute." After that, every once in a while, when asked, "Where is Father?" The child would answer, "In a minute."

Every night when it began to grow dark and still, the mother retied her obi sash and put into it a dagger in a shark-skin sheath. Then she tied the child to her back with a narrow obi, and went out softly through the wicket. The mother always wore straw sandals. The child was sometimes lulled to sleep on her back, listening to the rhythmic padding of those sandals.

Going west along the adobe walls of the neighbouring estates and down a gentle incline, there stands a big ginkgo tree. A turn to the right at the ginkgo tree leads one to a torii arch of stone, the gateway to a shrine a hundred metres beyond. With rice fields on one side and a low patch of dwarf bamboo on the other, one reaches the torii. Beyond the torii is a clump of dark cedars. Walking along the stone-paved path for another forty metres, one comes upon the stairs leading to the old shrine. Above the offertory box, weathered gray by the sun and rain, a pull-rope hangs down from the big wishing bell. In the daytime, one can see the wooden plaque inscribed with the name, "Hachiman-guu," the shrine of the god of war. The Japanese figure hachi (eight) is curiously formed, like two doves beak to beak. Nearby there are many framed pictures, mostly records of famous marksmen and their prowess with the arrow, plus an occasional sword, in dedication to the shrine.

Every time the child passes through the torii, it can hear an owl hooting in the top of a cedar. The child also hears the slap-slap of the mother's straw sandals on the paving stones. Then the sound stops as she rings the wishing bell and stoops down to clap her hands in the ritual way. Even the owl suddenly stops hooting. Then the mother prays to the gods with all her heart for her husband's safety. She has no doubt that Hachiman, the god of bow and arrow, will not leave unanswered her urgent prayer for her warrior husband.

At the sound of the bell the sleeping child often wakes up, and looks around, startled. Then it starts to cry on the mother's back, there in the darkness. She dandles the child, still murmuring her prayer. At times the crying stops, but sometimes it continues, loud and terrible. But the mother does not yet stand up.

On finishing her prayer at last, she walks up to the holy place, unties the narrow obi and slides the baby around from her back into her arms. She rubs her cheek tightly against the child's, saying "You're such a good baby. Wait here for a moment." After straightening out the tangles in the narrow obi, the mother ties one end around the child's waist and the other to the balustrade of the oratory. Then she goes down the stairs and paces back and forth a hundred times along the 40-metre stone-paved path, offering prayers.

It is lucky for the mother that her child, tied to the balustrade, can creep around the terrace of the oratory as far as the obi reaches. If the child sets up a cry, she tries to finish the prescribed hundred prayers quickly in her anxiety, but she loses her breath. When there is no other way, she interrupts herself, climbs up to the oratory where she hushes the child, and then starts over again from the beginning.

The father, whose safety the mother is so concerned about each night, has already been killed by a lordless warrior.

Such is the sad story I heard from my mother in my dream.

The Tenth Night

Ken-san came to tell me that Shoutarou unexpectedly came home that night, seven days after he had been taken off by a woman, and that, his temperature having suddenly risen, he is sick in bed.

Shoutarou is the best-looking young man in our neighbourhood and an extremely honest fellow, but he has a favourite pastime that may strike one as odd. When evening comes, he puts on his Panama hat, sits at the door of the fruit shop, and looks at the faces of the passing women, which never fail to entertain him. He never seems to want to do anything else.

When there are few women on the street, he turns to look at the fruit instead. All kinds of fruit. Peaches, apples, Japanese fruits, and bananas are beautifully served in baskets, arranged in two rows, so that the customers can easily select one for a present. Shoutarou looks at these baskets and says they are beautiful. He also says that if he were ever to enter a trade, a fruit shop would be just the thing for him. Nevertheless, he just sits there in his Panama hat and idles his time away.

Occasionally he comments on the fruit, saying that the colour of that Chinese citron, for example, is nice. Yet he has never bought any fruit, nor does he eat any free. He just extols the colour.

That evening a woman had unexpectedly stopped at the entrance of the store. Judging from what she was wearing, she seemed to be a woman of quality. The colour of her clothing caught Shoutarou's fancy. And her face, too, had a quality he found attractive, so Shoutarou saluted her in a courtly way by taking off his precious Panama hat. Then the woman pointed to the largest basket of fruit and asked him for it. Shoutarou quickly took it and handed it to her. When she tried to lift the basket, she remarked that it was a bit heavy for her.

As he was a man of leisure and very open-hearted by nature, Shoutarou offered to carry the basket to her house, and they left the shop together. He had been away ever since.

Easygoing as he always had been, this was going too far. While his friends and relatives were fretting over what they thought of as quite serious, Shoutarou suddenly came back on the night of the seventh day after he had gone away. People crowded around him and asked "Where have you been, Shou-san?" He merely replied that he had taken a train to the mountains.

It must have been a long train ride. According to what Shoutarou said, on getting off the train, he and the woman had come to a field. It was quite a large field, and wherever you looked, you could see only green grass. Walking along the grass, they suddenly came to the top of a huge precipice. Then the woman invited Shoutarou to jump off. Peering down, he could see the wall all right, but the bottom of it was too deep down to make out. Shoutarou, doffing his Panama hat, politely declined, again and again. The woman asked him whether he preferred to be licked by pigs, since he would not venture to jump off the precipice. Now Shoutarou hated pigs and Kumoemon the balladeer very much, but he thought that even not saving himself from either of these was worth the price of his life, and so could not bring himself to jump. Then a pig came grunting along. Shoutarou reluctantly hit the pig on its snout with a thin stick made of a betel palm. Giving a yelp, the pig tumbled down to the bottom of the cliff. While Shoutarou was still breathing a sigh of relief, another pig came towards him, rubbing him with its large snout. Shoutarou reluctantly swung the stick. With a yelp, the second pig followed the first headlong down the precipice. Then a third pig appeared. At that moment Shoutarou raised his eyes to discover, on the horizon where the green field ended, tens of thousands of grunting pigs trotting straight at him. He was terrified, but he could not stop tapping the snout of each pig one by one, gingerly, with the betel palm stick. Surprisingly, only a light touch of the stick to each snout sent the pigs easily over the cliff. Looking over the edge, he could see the pigs in an endless line, tumbling headfirst into the bottomless valley below. Thinking how many pigs he had dispatched to the bottom, Shoutarou began to feel afraid, and still the pigs came on and on and on. Like a swarming black cloud which had grown legs, continuously grunting, the pigs thrust their vigorous way through the green grass towards him, in a never-ending horde.

Shoutarou had tried desperately to keep up his courage, and for seven days and six nights he had gone on tapping pig snouts, until his arms got weak as a konnyaku jelly. Then one pig finally succeeded in licking him, and in the end, Shoutarou collapsed.

konnyaku jelly

Ken-san told me that story of Shoutarou and then advised me not to stare too much at the women. He is right, too, I find. Ken-san also mentioned that he would like to own Shoutarou's Panama hat.

It seems Shoutarou will not be saved. His Panama hat will be given to Ken-san.

Notes

The Second Night

Paper covered lamp (lantern)

"Andon," a small standing lamp made of iron or wood, with decorative grillwork designs on its four sides. Popular in the Edo period (1600-1868), when they were fuelled by oil or candles, some are now considered collectors' items. "Bombori" (see The Ninth Night) is a portable lantern with glass or paper covering its frame, and a hexagonal shade; sometimes used in a home as a permanent piece; may be carried by means of a bar attached horizontally at its base.

Buson

(1716-84). One of the three leading haiku poets of Japan, along with Basho (1644-94) and Issa (1763-1827); also known as Yosa Buson and Taniguchi Buson. Accomplished in the painting of the Bunjinga style, he developed the form called "haiga" or haiku sketch in Japanese art.

Kaichumonju
A Buddhist saint named Manjusri is the Bodhisattva
of wisdom and intellect; Kaichumonju is a painting
showing this Manjusri mounted on a lion, with four
followers, on a white cloud floating above an ocean.

Incense
Burned first as temple offerings before Buddhist
images, its use as a scent for upper-class homes and
clothing became fashionable even before the eighth
century.

Samurai
A member of the valiant warrior class in feudal times,
characterized by adherence to a very austere code of
honour.

Joshu (778-897)
A Chinese Zen priest.

Enlightenment
"Satori" or "Bodai" in Japanese; "Bodai" in Hindi. A
state of purely spiritual awakening characterized by
complete suspension of sense perception and of
desire.

Nothingness

In Chinese Taoist philosophy, a term for absolute non-existence seen as man's origin and final end; conceived in a Taoist reaction against the overly-practical direction of Confucian thought. The Taoist concept of nothingness blended with Indian Buddhism is found in Chinese and Japanese Buddhism, particularly in Zen Buddhism, in which nothingness is conceived as a transcendent absolute, going beyond existence as opposed to non-existence, and attainable by humans in an ideal state of enlightenment.

Alcove

"Tokonoma." A slightly raised alcove built into a Japanese tatami room for displaying decorative items such as calligraphy, flower arrangements, ceramic pieces, pictorial wall hangings, and other art objects; these are usually changed according to the season.

The Third Night

Hidarigakubo

The name of a place in Azabu ward (now Minato ward) in Tokyo.

Hottahara

The name of a place in the present Taito ward in Tokyo where there once stood an estate belonging to a warlord (daimyo) named Hotta.

Bonze priest

A Buddhist monk, especially of Japan or China; etymologically meaning "ordinary priest"; their heads are shaved as a sign of detachment from secular things, believed to be in imitation of Buddha who shaved his head after vowing to seek the path of holiness. A bald head is today described as "maru-bozu"; "bozu" is probably a corruption of the word "bonze."

Jizo

A popular Bodhisattva in Japan from the Heian period (794-1185) on, Jizo is depicted as a monk carrying a jewel and a staff; he is said to have vowed to help relieve all suffering beings, especially children and those in hell; legend sometimes crosses him with native deities. Stone figures of Jizo can often be seen in rice fields or along roads, dressed in cloth bibs by worshippers.

The fifth year of Bunka

The Bunka era (1804-1818) and the Bunsei era (1818-31) are often paired under the name Bunka and made to refer to the entire rule of the shogun Tokugawa Ienari (1787-1841); a time of relative tranquility politically and economically, but already showing signs of trouble ahead for the shogunate: rural and urban unrest and the foreign ships in Japanese waters which endangered the national policy of isolation; also a period of cultural and artistic achievement. Literature, drama, wood-printing, and haiku verse flowered; interest in the Western world became intense, and at the same time there was a resurgence of interest in Japanese classical learning.

The Year of the Dragon

Also known as "Eto." One year in the ancient Chinese system for dividing time and indicating directions, in which a complicated set of symbols, described metaphorically as ten trunks and twelve branches (jikkan jyunishi), are cross-combined into pairs that form a cycle of sixty. Their symbolism involves the concepts of yin and yang and the five elements of wood, fire, earth, metal and water. One method of naming these sets of twelve was to give each branch the name of an animal; this was applied to each in a cycle of twelve years according to the following order: ne (rat), ushi (ox), tora (tiger), u (hare), tatsu (dragon), mi (snake), uma (horse), hitsuji (ram or sheep), saru (monkey), tori (rooster), inu (dog), and i (boar); the system developed into a means of divination similar to astrology; hence "the Year of the Dragon" to indicate at which point in the cycle that the story takes place.

The Fourth Night

Nishime
A traditional dish containing ingredients such as burdock root, carrots, mushrooms, dried tofu, and other products from land and sea, which are simmered in soy sauce and sake.

Sake
An alcoholic brew made from rice fermented by malt; used to describe all alcoholic drinks. Refined sake, called seishu or nihonshu, is most commonly drunk in Japan; distilled sake is called shochu. Japanese made sake sometime after wet rice was introduced in 300 B.C.; the first written reference is from the third century A.D. First made in the imperial court or in large temples and shrines, and often associated with religious agricultural festivals, secular brewing began in the twelfth century; prohibition laws enacted from time to time were never really put into effect.

Shoji

Sliding screens made by spreading translucent paper sheets on latticed frames; used since the Heian period (794-1185) to divide rooms and corridors from rooms; the term formerly included the present fusuma, then called fusuma-shoji, sliding doors with opaque cloth and paper panels mounted in a wooden frame; now the word is used only for the paper and lattice version that admits light; shoji can be fitted on glass windows for interior decoration, though are less frequently seen in modern buildings.

Straw sandal

Waraji; a rough straw sandal with a thong separating the big toe from the second toe; worn strapped to the foot with straw bands that are laced across from one side to the other of the sole. A finer straw sandal is the zori, held on by the thong only. Made of straw, flax (asa) fibers, and wisteria or grape fibres, interwoven with bands of cloth; used for travel on foot. (See The Ninth Night)

The Fifth Night

Amanojaku

Also known as Amanojakko and Amanosagume. A nymph or demon of perversity which appears in folklore as a bane to thwart the plans and desires of humans. Used even now to describe a person who is contrary, habitually contradicting the ideas and desires of others. Figures found in Buddhist art and depicted as being trampled on by guardian deities, such as the Nio (see The Six Night).

The Sixth Night

Unkei (?-1223)

Sculptor of Buddhist images in the early Kamakura period (1185-1333); the greatest master of the Kei school of sculpture who revitalized the art with his strong, dynamic style which won him popularity among the warriors of his time; works include the Dainichi Nyorai at Enjoji in Nara as well as three treasured figures at Jorakuji in Yokosuka, Kanagawa Prefecture.

Nio

A pair of benevolent deities believed to guard temple gates; the figures in the story were carved in wood in the Nara workshop of Unkei and his colleague Kaikei (from late twelfth to early thirteenth century) and are considered among the best; they stand, more than 800 centimetres tall, before the south gate of the temple Todaiji in Nara.

Ken

A unit of measurement; 5.965 feet

Rickshaw

"Jinrikisha." Literally, man-powered vehicle; a two-wheeled cart pulled by a man; said to be inspired by the Western horse-drawn carriage; originally a simple contraption of a canopy placed over a wagon by means of four poles, it later developed into a more elegantly elaborate carriage; used now only as a picturesque tourist attraction.

Yamatotakeru no Mikoto

Prince Yamatotakeru; a legendary hero supposed to be the son of a twelfth century legendary emperor, Keiko; he seems to be the embodiment of the archetypal hero figure, thought to have emerged in Japan somewhere between the fifth and seventh centuries; the story of this prince is chronicled in Kojiki (712) and Nihon Shoki (720), where heroic acts and a major role in the mid-seventh century growth of the Yamato State are attributed to him. His tale rings with the knightly valour, epic deeds, and magical elements of all such poetic legends.

Meiji (1867-1912)
Meiji jidai, the period marking the reign of Emperor
Meiji and the beginning of Japan as a modern state;
begun when the young emperor Mutsuhito, age sixteen,
named his rule Meiji, which means Enlightenment
Reign; the name was applied to him, according to
the Japanese custom for emperors after death.

Sun
A unit of measurement; 1.193 inches.

The Eighth Night

Awa rice cake
"Mochi"; a glutinous type of rice, steamed and pounded
to a resilient mass and shaped into mounds or squares;
soft enough to be eaten fresh, it hardens when dry
and must be softened by grilling or in a special soup
(Zoni); sometimes made with millet or mixed with
certain herbs or other ingredients; also used in a
variety of sweets, often with sweet red bean paste;
associated with traditional rituals and festivals such as
New Year's Day and Children's Day (May 5); originally
used as a religious offering as well as food; the traditional
process of making it by hand involves mortar and
mallet, strong men, and a rhythmic motion of hands—

at risk of being struck by the mallet if the rhythm is broken—as they extract portions of the mochi for moulding into mounds; an exciting festival ritual.

Bean curd

"Tofu"; first made in China around the first century and introduced into Japan in the seventh century; rich in protein, easy to digest and inexpensive; made from soybeans in a process that yields a soft, off-white, slightly jellied substance that is cut into brick-like squares; a cotton cloth lining on the bottom of the tank where the tofu settles, and by which it is delicately lifted, imprints a coarse grain to the bottom surface that gives it the name momengoshi (momen=cotton); another, smoother variety substitutes a finer cloth and is called kinugoshi (kinu=silk). Tofu is eaten in many different dishes such as soup or sukiyaki, or simply alone with some flavoured topping like green onions, soy sauce, grated ginger, or other tasty addition.

Root of shimada

One of many women's hair styles fashionable in the late Edo period (1600-1868), Meiji (1868-1912) and Taisho (1912-26), such as gingko style and ichogaeshi.

Geisha

Literally, "artist"; traditional female entertainers who offer song, dance, conversation, games, and companionship to customers in certain restaurants; the world of the geisha is described as the "karyukai." In the 1920s geisha numbered about 80,000, and in the 1980s only 10,000; the decline is attributed to the gradual replacement of the geisha by Western-style bar hostesses who do not require the rigorous and costly training of the geisha.

Goldfish

"Kingyo," *Carassius auratus* in Latin. Probably bred in 11th-century China from the freshwater fish known as crucian carp and brought to Japan in the sixteenth and seventeenth centuries, becoming popular in the early 1800s; exported by Japan to the United States at the turn of the century, trade fell off as American goldfish breeding improved; over 20 varieties are now bred in Japan.

The Ninth Night

The prescribed hundred prayers

Hyakudo mairi; a custom originating in the Heian period (794-1185), according to which prayers are repeated 100 times, either in 100 daily pilgrimages to a shrine or temple or reciting the prayers in one hundred continuous rounds within the shrine or temple grounds; usually performed at night or in the early hours so as not to be seen by anyone, which the pilgrim believed would result in the petition not being granted.

Obi

The long sash worn with traditional Japanese kimono. Before the eight century, a narrow obi was used to secure the waist of the loose garments of the time; with new weaving techniques from Korea and China during the Nara period (710-794), it became more elegant, but its use by court ladies in the Heian period (794-1185) disappeared until the end of the fifteenth century, when the fashion was revived. The man's obi of today, a narrow band of soft gray or black silk, is tied a little below the waist in the back. Women's obi today are stiff, as wide as 20 cm and over three metres long; when used for formal wear they can be colourful, elaborately woven or embroidered cloth, and costly, more precious even than the kimono; in early times married women wore their obi tied at the front, but now the obi is always tied at the back in shapes ranging from very simple to quite fanciful bows.

Torii

A stylized Tao-like arch, which stands before or inside a Shinto shrine compound, serving as an entrance to the holy place as well as the symbol for a shrine. Originally constructed of wood, stone began to be used during the Heian period (794-1185) as well as copper, porcelain and, in modern times, also concrete. Its form consists of two columns topped by two over-reaching bars placed one below the other, leaving a proportionate space between; the lower bar penetrates and protrudes from the pillars.

Hachimangu

A popular Shinto deity, the spirit of legendary emperor Ojin, believed to protect warriors as well as the community at large; legend has it that Hachiman provided protection for the construction of the Great Buddha (Daibutsu) in Nara (749) for which he was given the title Daibosatsu (Great Bodhissattva) and regarded as a protector of the religion. The Hachiman cult became important in Kyoto and in Kamakura where it was established by Yoritomo Minamoto (1147-99), founder of the Kamakura shogunate (1192-1333). There are 25,000 Hachiman shrines in Japan today.

Shrine

Jinja; an enclosed area with a sanctuary and several out-buildings for practice of the Shinto religion; the main buildings usually consist of a main sanctuary (honden) where a sacred object personifying the deity or deities is housed and which only priests may enter, and a hall of worship (haiden) where rituals are conducted and people can make their offerings. Worshippers invoke the deities residing there by standing in front of the building, clapping their hands and ringing a bell that is sounded by a pull on a thick rope hanging from the rafters; offerings of money are placed in the wood-slatted offertory box; entrance to the building by laymen is permitted only for certain rituals. Near the haiden of a typical shrine is the purification place (temizuya), where visitors rinse their hands, a shelter for portable shrines (mikoshi) used in processions and festivals, a hall for preparing food offerings, a miniature shrine for protecting the main shrine, and an office where amulets are sold. Some shrines form a network with other affiliated shrines throughout the country; others are local and independent.

The Tenth Night

Kumoemon

Tochuken Kumoemon (1873-1916); real name,

Houkichi Okamoto; a balladeer of the Meiji and Taisho periods who became popular after a performance in Tokyo in 1907 (Meiji 40); the samisen, an instrument with three strings of cat-gut, customarily accompanied such chanting.

Konnyaku Jelly

A non-caloric paste made from a tuberous root (devil's tongue; konjak, konnyaku, amorphophallus) and moulded into resilient blocks or shaped into noodles; used in a variety of simmered dishes (nimono see The Forth Night) and in sukiyaki.

Translators

The First and Second Nights: Takumi KASHIMA, Professor of English Department at Nagasaki College of Foreign Languages.

The Third and Fourth Nights: Kyoko NONAKA, Lecturer of English at Kyushu Institute of Information Sciences.

The Fifth and Sixth Nights: Hideki OIWA, Associate Professor of English Department at Nagasaki College of Foreign Languages.

The Seventh and Eighth Nights: Hirokatsu KAWASHIMA, Associate Professor of English Department at Nagasaki College of Foreign Languages.

The Ninth and Tenth Nights: Katsunori FUJIOKA, Associate Professor of English Department at Nagasaki College of Foreign Languages.

English Consultants

Notes and Comments by Takumi KASHIMA and Loretta Rose LORENZ, Professors of English Department at Nagasaki College of Foreign Languages.

⑤ Soseki Museum in London

80b, The Chase, London SW4
Tel: +44(0)20-7720-8718
Fax: +44(0)20-8773-9670
Email: Nsoseki@aol.com
http://www.dircon.co.uk/soseki-museum/info.html

Hours
February - September
Wednesday & Saturday   10:00 - 12:00 / 14:00 - 17:00
Sunday   14:00 - 17:00

Admission
Adult £4 Student £3 Child £2

Japan Books in London

• Largest quality stock of books,
old photographs,
documents on Japan
• Booksearches service

Shop : Japan Books (Y&S Co., Ltd.)
C/o. Biblion
1-7, Davies Mews, London W1Y 2LP
Underground: Bond Street (Central Line)

Monday - Friday 10:00 - 18:00
Saturday 11:00 - 17:00

Postal Address:
Japan Books (Y&S Co., Ltd.)
P. O. Box 693, Carshalton, Surrey SM5 3ZN UK
Tel: +44(0)20-8773-2576/ Mobile: 0956-499259
Fax: +44(0)20-8286-8003
http://www.yandscompany.co.uk/japanbooks.htm
Email: Jbooksuk@aol.com

Printed in the United States
by Baker & Taylor Publisher Services